GABRIELLE'S

HEART

An Angel's Touch

by

ESMERALDA LINTNER

ISBN-13 978-1794482449
First printing February 2019

Printed in the United States of America

Dedicated To

All Of Our

GUARDIAN ANGELS

INTRODUCTION

Far above the cosmos, skies, stars and galaxies, way up into the heavenlies where all the angelic hosts live is where you will find me. No war, strife or human suffering is allowed. All is a calm, peaceful coexistence. It is where harmony, beauty, and love radiate their glowing power of eternal bliss. No presence of those of the flesh may exist with us here. The Almighty of all creation lives here, and all souls are satisfied. You may have either read or heard about us with our white bodies and clothes appropriate for our genders. Some say we speak very dramatically, lofty --- in King James Version. The earth dwellers give us such a majestic image as if we are far superior to them, and as though we cannot relate to you humans.

Far be it! I know, for I am one of those beings.

Hi there, my friend! Let me introduce myself. I'm Gabrielle and it's so nice to meet you. In my life's travels upon the earth I have met people with problems that really needed my attention. Believe me, there were many. There are a few special cases that touched my very soul: love, relationships, self-image, just to mention a few.

You can believe me: we angels are busy, too. There are many humans to attend to. I am so glad and thrilled that you have chosen this time from your earthly existence to be with me. Sit back and listen to the stories I will tell.

1

ONE

My first case was between two lovers: Allison and Raphael. Little did they know that one day they would meet. Both had image problems and lack of self- confidence. It's the usual thing I have heard time and time again:

"I don't look pretty or handsome enough."

I will take you back through times past. We shall time travel together through your human minds.

It was on a calm sunny day. Allison was now twenty-three and living with her parents, John and Judy White, on an average-sized farm in the Midwest. The parents were in their living room, both quite concerned for their daughter's future.

"I wonder if my daughter will ever get married. Will I ever become a grandmother?" *Judy White was in quite a fretful mood.*

"Don't worry dear," *John comforted her.* "She is only twenty-three." *Scratching his head, he added*, "Come to think of it, I would love to be a grandfather myself."

The mother went over to a nearby table, opened a drawer and took out some photos of their daughter. They looked them over. Her mom was a real worrywart, more so than the father. I couldn't understand why, because those two always went to church. Don't they know their religion tells them not to worry?

Allison was in her bedroom upstairs daydreaming, wondering when her true love would come. I will never forget that day she began talking to herself:

"I guess I'll never get married. I'm not that pretty. Why, even the boys in town avoid me! Even in high school no one asked me to the prom. I must be so ugly and a bore to boot. Life is just the pits, and shitty, too!"

After hearing this it really grabbed my attention. Such a lovely girl, and she was putting herself down. It's a shame. I have heard this more times than I care to count. When will these humans ever learn? Anyway, it looked like another job for Super Gabrielle! (See, I have a sense of humor, too!)

That afternoon, I decided to pay a visit to her. When I appear to a human, it's not in person or through some mystic vision. It's very subtle. I simply make my presence known: a cool gentle breeze. On this particular day I chose to make her dying flower come alive.

"Oh, my God! I don't believe it, my flower came alive. There seems to be a cool breeze, and it's blowing all around me."

For my next feat, I just whispered into her mind, or spirit, as you earthlings call it. I simply whispered:

Why are you putting yourself down?

to which she replied in thoughts communicated to me, "I have accomplished quite a bit in my life. I

3

graduated at the top of my class, and now work as the secretary to the president of the biggest bank in town."

Then I heard Allison sort of digress a bit and go into her carnal mind. "A man would be nice, but that's not all there is to life. I would love to shack up with one right now! They sure are hot. I'd love to have one plow me."

She made me laugh. That girl is something else! Go, Girl!

Across town there was a young man named Raphael. He worked as a grocery clerk at the local market, "Smitherson's." He did not make very much, just enough to get by. He did have plans to attend community college and major in business. Raphael had a dream to one day start his own chain of stores. He was twenty-five with light brown hair and a small mustache. He had a very slim but muscular build and a very kind countenance about him. He too daydreamed about a lovely lady coming along and marrying him.

But alas, just like Allison, another excuse. He believed that he was not wealthy enough. He lived as a loner, a recluse. The poor guy went along with this lie most of his young life until one day I paid a visit to him. He was at home fixing dinner for himself. I just waved my magic wings and the lights in his apartment went off and on.

"What the hell is going on? Maybe there is some

kind of an electrical problem in here."

Then, I got in a little mischievous. I simply floated on over to his CD player, touched it and it came on. I knew by scanning his mind that he loved country music and decided to activate the song, "Kiss an Angel Good Morning."

"Hey! How did that happen? This CD just went on by itself. Oh, this is one of my favorite songs from Charley Pride. Those oldies are still the greatest."

Raphael was drawn to the music. He sat on his couch and listened to it. As he was relaxing and taking in the lyrics, I very softly spoke to his mind. He began to reflect on what he was hearing.

"Boy, if had a girl right now, I would kiss her, treat her like my own angel and have some nice hot sex when I got home."

It looked like his hormones were working overtime. It didn't surprise me. He was exactly like any healthy male. I could tell he had a rather heavenly gift.

"I have a nice one for her. She'll just love every inch of it." *He sounded like a typical human with a one track mind. It made me laugh.* "I sure hope that someday a nice cute chick will fall for me. Hopefully, she will take me just as I am. She has to be a special girl!"

It looked like I was getting through to him. I proceeded to check what else I had in my bag of tricks. Get it? I could see Felix the Cat laughing at that one!

On Thursday of the following week Raphael was hard at work, checking out his customers. While he finished up with the line of people, there stood Allison waiting to be served. Raphael took an immediate liking to her. He couldn't keep his eyes off her and tried not to be too obvious. Allison smiled back in return. She also noticed how handsome he was.

"Is that all for today, Miss?' *he asked*.

Being a little shy Allison replied, "Yes, but I'll need some help putting the bags of groceries in my car."

"Why, I'd love to do that for you. I'm free. I'll just close the line and be right with you."

Well! Raphael wasted no time. He darted out the door to make sure he was there for her. Both of them smiled at each other. Allison blushed and it matched her rosy red cheeks.

"How are you today?"

"I'm fine," *she responded with a little giggle*.

"Are you new in town?"

"No! I live about five minutes from here."

"Funny. I never saw you before. I'm Raphael. What's your name?"

"I'm Allison." *Still blushing, she smiled. At this point I could see something begin to develop. Both of them stood silently, waiting for the one to ask the other out. How do I know this? Because we angels can also read minds. I guess this was the time for my bag of tricks. I simply spoke to Raphael's mind*:

Remember the song, "Kiss an Angel Good Morning?"

Now's your chance.
Ask her out!

The poor guy needed a little prodding. I spoke again:

Go ahead, don't miss this big chance!

Raphael got a little nervous and tongue-tied. "W-w-would you like to g-g-go out s-s-sometime?"
Allison was taken by surprise. She didn't know what to think. I know this because I heard her thoughts. Being rather shy, she answered, "I think I'd like to."
Raphael couldn't believe that she had actually agreed. "How about tonight? Will you be hungry? I know a nice place across town, 'The Blue Bird Café.'"
"That sounds great. I'd love to go there with you."
"If you tell me where you live, I could come by for you, say, about six-ish?"
"Okay." *She drove away from the supermarket parking lot, brimming with enthusiasm. It looked like something was brewing. I decided I should be there just in case they would need a little oomph!*
That evening Raphael drove up in front of the White's home. He got out of his car and as he approached the door he almost wanted to turn back and cancel the whole visit. He was starting to get cold feet because of his inferiority complex.
Well, here we go again. I'll just whisper a little

confidence to him. Go ahead, you can do it! She's all yours. Don't be afraid, just knock. Your lovely angel is awaiting you. Allison's parents are excited that she had a date!

He finally got up his courage and knocked. Mr. White opened the door and stood there. "Yes may I help you, young man?"

"I'm Raphael. Is Allison ready?"

"Why, yes! Come on in, she'll be right down."

"It's nice to meet you, sir."

"Thank you, likewise. I'd like you to meet Allison's mother, my wife Judy."

She greeted him with a warm welcome. "Hello, Raphael. It's nice to meet you. I'm so glad that you're taking our daughter out tonight."

"Thank you, Mrs. White. We're going out for some dinner, and then maybe take in the town a little."

Mr. White looked him over and told him, "Whatever you do, take good care of Allison."

"Oh, I promise I will. She is a special lady."

Both parents were laughing and smiling as their daughter came downstairs. Raphael couldn't keep his eyes off her. She was wearing a white skirt trimmed with roses and a lavender sweater with sequins sparkling all over.

"My, you're looking lovely this evening, Allison."

"Why, thank you, Raphael. You're looking handsome yourself."

The father laughed. "OK, you two! Go out and enjoy yourself. Don't do anything that I wouldn't do."

Allison looked back at her father and rolled her eyes. "Oh, Daddy! You're such a comic, aren't you?"

Leaving the house, they headed for Raphael's car. He opened the door for Allison to let her in before going over to the driver's side. Allison's parents watched and were impressed.

"I can tell that he's a real gentleman. It's hard to find one these days."

"Yeah, and that 2000 Camaro he has isn't bad either."

"Ha! It figures you'd notice the car and not be concerned about your daughter's date."

The couple drove to "The Blue Bird Café." The both really enjoyed the meal, not to mention each other [hahaha!] After leaving the restaurant Raphael really got his courage up.

"How would you like to take an evening drive? I know a nice place near where the lake is."

"That sounds cool. I'd love to, Raphael."

They drove for a few miles and arrived at Swan Lake. The night was young, and both love as well as sexual arousal were in the air. They stopped at the lake's edge, and he leaned over to kiss her. Soon they were making love and some other things began to arise. Allison raised her skirt and guided Raphael's hand up it. He pulled back at first, but then went for all the gusto he could get. It was a night that neither of them would soon forget.

They saw more of each other as the months went

by. Soon they were madly in love and decided to get married.

They chose the Fourth of July as their wedding date which was a special day to do it. They were married at the Episcopal Church in town. Everyone came and the Whites were especially thrilled. Their daughter finally had a husband. Allison soon became the vice president of the bank due to all her hard work and promotions. Raphael left "Smitherson's" when he was offered a position as regional manager for a chain of "Robertson's Supermarkets." They both attributed their success to their marriage and the love they had for one another.

But I say that a little angel's touch also goes a long way, wouldn't you agree?

TWO

I recall another case which needed my heavenly help, you might say. This was about Cindy Caughman who was a real estate agent. She was in her late thirties and felt so lonely. Cindy spent most of her time just immersing herself in her work. She spent many a lonely night by herself. There were times that she became depressed. It looked like she was trying to ignore her real problem: love and a man in her life. Her sex life was down the drain as far as she was concerned. Such a busy beaver, but no time for Cupid to strike with his bow to open her heart to receive a person's love.

One night I decided to pay a visit to her bedroom. I could hear her innermost thoughts. "I am tired of this life, it's so fast paced. I feel so lonely with no man around. But who am I fooling? My work takes up too much of my time. I guess that I'll be a lonely old maid the rest of my life."

It looked like another job for Gabbie! I gave her thoughts about going on her internet. She used it quite a lot. It's amazing what you humans come up with these days. I ever so gently guided her hands on over to a dating service. She came upon one which grabbed her fancy.

"Mmm! This one looks pretty fantastic. It says that you can view video clips of some eligible bachelors. And it looks like there is a wide variety of men. It says they are having a free promotion. I'll just sign up here. I've never done this before. I wonder what will happen…"

Cindy took her time watching several videos put together by different guys. After she went through at least a dozen men she was frustrated and was going to hang it all up. Using my heavenly intuition, I prodded her to give it one more good ol' college try. And sure enough! One man caught her attention. His name was Ryan York and he lived in Brentwood, California. He worked for an advertising agency in the promotion department. She was immediately drawn to him, not only by what he did for a living, but also his looks.

"Wow, he's 40?! He looks a lot younger than that. He states that he has the same problem: too much work, not enough dating. I'll bet he'd be hot in bed, too!"

It looks like you humans have a one track mind. I don't blame her. If I were single and pretty like her, I'd want a nice hot young man myself. Heh-heh-heh!

She looked and saw that there was still the free trial which she could take advantage of. Cindy could leave an interest in his emails. It would signal an alert to him.

The next day she received an exciting email in her box. He replied back to her, wanted to know more about her and possibly meet. She quickly made a video of herself and posted it to his inbox.

Well! The next morning she arose and went to check her emails. Sure enough, there was an email from Ryan. He left his phone number and wanted to hear from her. She was all atwitter and couldn't wait to call and meet him. She made sure she called him at a good hour which was before she left for work at nine-thirty a.m. She let it ring a couple of times.

"Hello?" *This was her big moment*.

"Hi, is this Ryan?"

"Yes it is," *he answered in a very masculine sounding voice.*

"This is Cindy Caughman. You asked me to give you a call."

"Why yes, Cindy! It sure is good to hear from you. I just love your video and what you shared with me. Are you free either tonight or sometime this week?"

"Yes, I am. Tomorrow night will be fine."

"I would love to have dinner with you at 'Foxes Inn.'"

"Wow! That is really an elegant restaurant."

"It is rather a plush place to eat. It's all for a special lady like yourself. How about six?"

"That would be fine," *she replied, full of excitement*.

"Great! See you then."

The next evening they met at the restaurant where they wined and dined the night away. They both loved being with each other. He even invited her out to catch a movie the next night. Of course she was more than willing.

Having been out to see the movie on the second date, Cindy was invited to his nice condominium in

Brentwood. The rest of the evening was filled with glasses of wine coupled with sizzling hot romance. They held each other, kissed intermittently while drinking their wine and listened to soft classical music. They finally made their way over to his bedroom, where of course something else took place as in a three letter word: it begins with S and ends with X.

If you're good at crossword puzzles you already know it was SEX!

They slowly took each other's clothes off and continued with their kissing. He began sucking on her nipples and she ever so gently rubbed the head of his large --- ahmm! --- cock. [*I think I'm being a naughty little angel, aren't I?*]

"Do you have a condom?" *she asked breathlessly.*

"Why, I sure do. It's right her just for a special occasion."

Cindy then asked to examine the package of condoms. "Oooh! This one is wild cherry!" *She slipped in on his ever so hardening cock.* "Let me taste a little and see how wild it is. *She began sucking.* "Mmm… tastes good," *she moaned. He went inside of her and they screwed the night away.*

Isn't that funny, two horny workaholics going at it! It figures; love and sex will do it every time. They both fell in love and saw a lot more of each other. Who knows what's in store for these two lonely lovebirds. Maybe little birdies? [*Tweet tweet!*]

THREE

Let me share with you another case. This one is much different than the previous ones you just read. It's about a married couple. This was between Andy and Arleen Herts. Both of them lived in San Diego. They had a nice house. They had also rented a lovely beach house as well. They were both in their early forties and had been a happy couple for quite some time.

But as they grew older together it seemed that the spark of romance was beginning to wane. It looked like the ole flame was burning out! They didn't spend much time talking or making love. In fact, they both were thinking of seeing someone else.

How could this be? They both had a nice home and good paying jobs. Arleen was a defense lawyer, and Andy was a doctor who had a private practice. But their love lives were drifting apart.

One day they almost broke up. Arleen found a receipt for an overnight stay at a Days Inn. It was dated for the day before and Andy had said he had been working late.

My goodness, what an evil web you humans do weave: shame, shame!

The following morning, she confronted him at the breakfast table. "Andy?"

"Yes, Hon?" *he replied in a calm, understanding voice.*

"Don't give that 'Hon' act," *she snapped.*

15

He looked surprised and did not expect her to react in that tone of voice.

"Why? What's wrong?"

"Don't act so innocent with me, you lying sack of shit!" [*My, my! What language you human use when you're mad*!] "I thought you were working late last night."

"I was."

"You snake in the grass! It just so happens I found a sales slip marked PAID for one night at the Days Inn. Who were you shacking up with, some young chick probably in her early thirties or younger?" *She began to sob uncontrollably.*

"I was going to tell you, but I did meet this girl. She was a patient of mine. She was lonely, so I wanted to cheer her up."

"A likely story! So what did you do, fuck her?"

"Yes, but I didn't love her as much as I do you!"

"My God! You're fucking your own patients?!"

"Calm down. This one was just a one night stand."

"A one night stand?!" *she yelled.* "Have there been others?"

"Just three others.

"Three?!?"

"Don't get upset. It was only physical, nothing else. I have no deep feelings for any woman except you."

"Besides your young hot chick patient, who the hell were the other two?"

"Only two of the nurses from the hospital."

Arleen was mad as hell. [Oh! Forgive me that little slip of the angelic tongue.] "What did you do, stick a thermometer up their asses?"

"No, but I stuck something else in them --- my cock."

She yelled at him and wouldn't stop yelling. It looked like it was time for damage control. Your friendly neighborhood marriage counselor was on her way! That evening, I decided to pay a visit to her. She felt all alone with no one to talk to.

Arleen could not understand that this had actually happened to her. Her marriage had lasted five years with this man and he had been cheating on her. She sat on the edge of her bed, trying to hold back her tears, mostly in vain. At that moment I arrived on the scene.

I heard her talking out loud to herself. "What did I do? Where did I go wrong? Haven't I been fulfilling his needs?"

The poor girl really touched my heart, for it was broken. It looked like it was time for some mending. I stood by her bed, waving a few times with my wings and hands. The room was filled with a cool breeze. Even Arleen commented, "Boy, where is my sweater? It's suddenly cold in here!

On her nightstand there was a phone book. With my powers I knocked the book off the table, forcing a page wide open. She picked it up and noticed the page in question. It was for MARRIAGE COUNSELORS. I spoke to her mind in a soft whisper:

17

Try this person; he's close to where you live.

'Hmm...! This one looks real close to me, he's Dr. Brett Cummings. It says that he specializes in marriage and sexual problems. I don't know if I should. I've never called a counselor for our kind of problem before."

I gently whispered to her:

Go ahead, you have nothing to lose.
Don't be afraid, there are others just like you.

She finally got up the nerve, and gave Dr. Cummings a call.

"Hello, is this Dr. Brett Cummings's office?"

"Yes it is, how may I help you?"

"I have a marriage problem and would like to speak to him."

"Why, yes. This is his receptionist. I can make an appointment for you. How is next week?"

"No, this is an emergency. Do you have anything sooner?"

"Let me see,... He has one opening tomorrow morning at around eleven a.m. Would that be fine with you?"

"Yes, that would be OK."

"Do you have our address?"

"Yes, I do, and I'll see you in the morning."

"That's fine, and may I ask your name?"

"It's Mrs. Arleen Herts."

"We will see you then."

That night was another lonely one for her. Her husband came home late again: two in the morning. He took his clothes off and jumped into bed with her, but she was fast asleep.

The next morning she headed out to her appointment with Dr. Cummings. She was feeling very nervous and full of anxiety. When she arrived she gave her name and waited for him. He came out of his office, greeted her and invited her in. He was in his early fifties with medium black hair, a medium build and a bushy mustache.

"Mrs. Herts? Please come right on in." *He made her feel relaxed and right at home.* "Would you care to join me in a cup of coffee? I just brewed a fresh pot."

"Yes, please, with just a little cream and no sugar."

"There you are, Mrs. Herts. Now, how may I help you?"

She lost her composure and moist tears began forming in her eyes. "My husband and I are having problems. I found out he was cheating on me with someone --- three 'someones,' as a matter of fact. I had to drag it out of him. We have been together now for five years."

Arleen continued with her story about how they had drifted apart. She was afraid they might wind up getting a divorce. The doctor scribbled notes as she

19

spoke. She continued talking for about two hours. Afterwards, she felt much better. He gave some ideas to help her and her husband grow closer to one other. Primarily she had to get his attention through foreplay and the use of sex toys.

"I see! Maybe we should go on a trip somewhere together."

"That's right. Show him that he doesn't need another woman and that only you can fulfill his needs."

"Should I try and get him to come along with me to see you, too?"

"Yes! That would be a very good idea. It would be good to see you both together."

That evening Andy came home and looked around to see where Arleen was. He called for her. She stood at the top of the stairs wearing a see-through night gown and then slowly descended.

"My, you're looking very sexy tonight darling."

She put her arms around him and they kissed each other for a few moments.

"How was your day?"

"It was fine. I had lots of cases." *She asked him to sit down because she wanted to have a talk with him about something which was very important. She reached to put her arms around him again.*

"Honey, I am concerned for the both of us. Something seems to be separating you and me. I decided to visit a marriage counselor and got some good advice from him."

He pulled back and was angry with her. "I don't need a shrink, nothing is wrong with either of us." *She also tried to hold back her temper and suggested he come along with her next time. He again rejected the idea, but she would not drop the matter.*

"If you don't come with me next time, I no longer want to live with you. I'll just pack my bags and we will separate. Eventually I'll want a divorce on the basis of infidelity and mental cruelty."

He was very surprised how serious she was, and it shook him up quite a bit. She also insisted that he quit, as she put it, SCREWING AROUND. She convinced him that she was indeed serious and wanted their marriage to work. He put his arms around her and told her that he understood.

The following week, they went together to see Dr. Cummings, and through therapy they slowly got back into loving each other again. They even went on a second honeymoon to, of all places, Berlin, Germany, because neither of them had ever been there. The day they went on their trip I personally spoke to Andy's mind:

Remember, stay faithful and don't ever let her go. You need nothing else.

Well, several years have passed, and they now have two children. The moral to this story is: When the love light begins flicker, act fast and rekindle it!

FOUR

This next story is an interesting one. It deals with living in a delusional world of self. May I present to you Lisa Towers....

She was thirty-five and had always been single. Lisa spent many hours gazing into her mirror and worshiping herself. She thought the world revolved around her, not even taking time out for love.

Well, she was in for a big surprise. I was going to be there to turn her world upside down. You are about to enter into Gabrielle's Zone! [Get it? Even we angels love classic TV!]

Our story takes place in Hollywood where Lisa resided. She spent lots of time going to Hollywood parties and trying to be noticed, but everyone seemed to avoid her. I wonder, why? Can you guess?

On one particular evening she had been invited to a girlfriend's birthday party. The problem was that she was invited by accident. Somehow her name had been transferred to the list of invitees.

Well, she was about to get a real eye opener. She made sure that she had on the finest of clothes and makeup for the evening. "Wait until they get a load of this! All eyes will be on me," *she thought to herself. She fully intended to be the belle of the ball. When she arrived, they looked up the name on the list. Sure enough, it* was *on there.*

"Come on in, my name is Jack Berger," *the host said. She immediately started to flirt and tried to get him to notice how pretty she looked. She was expecting a compliment, but he said nothing.*

Lisa walked into the main salon and waited for somebody to say something about how she looked, but they just ignored her. There was even some gossip circulating that she was there.

"Oh no! Look who it is!"

"They invited *her*?"

"She's got the biggest ego in town."

"Stay away from her."

"She'll talk your head off all night."

"Yeah, and it'll be all about herself."

"What a bore."

"She thinks she's Princess Grace."

"Fancies herself as the reincarnation of Marilyn Monroe."

Lisa tried to make friends, but when she started talking it was all about her new clothes and her looks. Before you know it, they all began disappearing on her. This went on for most of the evening. She was getting rather depressed, not knowing why they were all trying to stay away from her. She walked out towards one of the balconies and there she overheard some of the girls talking.

"Who invited Lisa to the party?"

"Lisa who?"

"Lisa Towers."

"Oh, you mean that girl who everyone says is such a bore?"

"No one wants to be around her."

"All she ever does is talk about herself."
"It's all about her."
"She is not even married."
"No wonder. What man would want her?"
"She would bore any man to death!"

They all laughed and continued with their socializing. Poor Lisa, she had received a rude awakening. She wanted to cry and just leave the party. It's a good thing I was there. I considered what kind of a love spell I could cast. At that moment I saw a nice handsome young man standing by himself. I flitted over toward him and began speaking to his mind.

See that nice young lady?
She looks all alone.
Why don't you go over
and introduce yourself?

Lisa caught the young gentleman's eye. He found himself becoming very attracted to her. He strolled over to where she was. "Good day, how are you? Are you enjoying yourself?"

Lisa was taken by surprise that any man would even be interested in her. "The party is so full of interesting people, one can get lost here."

"Well, I certainly am interested in you. You are very pretty."

"Thank you." *She blushed as red as her cheeks.*

"Oh, my name is Steven Roberts. What's yours?"

"I'm Lisa Towers. Thank you for coming over to see me. No one has even said 'boo' to me!"

"Well, that's not nice. Such a lovely lady should have someone to be with. I'll be happy to be your escort for this party." *Steven was a very attractive man. He was six feet tall with blue eyes, black hair and a muscular build.*

"Why, thank you. You're put together rather nicely, too."

Steven felt rather complimented. "Thank you! I work out at the gym on a regular basis. Would you care for some refreshments?"

She was very impressed with Steven They held hands and proceeded to get some drinks. As she walked over to the bar, all the other women stared at both Steven and her.

"Look! Who's that guy Lisa is with?"

"Wow! Where did she get him?"

Lisa proudly paraded around the room with Steven. All the other girls started getting jealous of her. She just gave them a little wink as she walked past.

"What will you have Lisa?"

"I'll have Scotch on the rocks."

"OK, sounds good, I'll have the same." *Steven ordered for the both of them.*

"Would you care to step out on the balcony again?"

"I'd love to, Mister Roberts."

"You don't have to be so formal. Just call me Steven."

25

They both looked over the edge of the balcony, holding hands at first and then putting their arms around each other, followed by the first kiss.

"Do you like my new dress and hair?"

"Yes I do. It makes you looks so lovely and sexy!"

"Thank you." *Lisa began talking and focusing on herself again. She didn't notice how Steven was reacting, so I gave her a little nudge and whispered to her*:

Remember what the other girls said.
You're talking too much about yourself.
Put the attention on Steven,
otherwise
you're going to turn him off!

"By the way, you do look very handsome. I like men with muscles." *Steven smiled and Lisa began gently rubbing his arms.*

"Thanks. I try to keep in shape." *They kissed again and found themselves becoming very attracted to one another.* "Say! I have an idea. Would you like to go for a ride up in the hills?"

Lisa immediately perked up. "I would love to."

They both left the party and walked out to Steven's car. It was a Fiat. He opened the passenger side for Lisa, she arranged herself comfortably in the passenger seat and soon they drove off. Reaching the top of the highest hill, they looked out at the view over the city.

"It's very romantic being up here with you."

"That's right. Just you and me, babe."

They kissed over and over, and soon --- oops! --- I saw a little petting. I spoke very softly to both of their minds:

Better be careful.
You're in a public place,
and there are the cops, you know!

They both looked at each other and realized they had gotten too carried away. Steven turned on the radio and the song "Love Turns You Around" was playing.

"Oh! I just love that song, it's so romantic." *They kissed and loved the night away.*

Exit Lisa Towers, once a self-absorbed woman who discovered that there is more to life than herself. She found that love is the key. It can only be found with me, right here in GABES ZONE!

FIVE

This next tale is rather interesting. It's about a gentlemen who is sort of a playboy; somehow he never settled down, always chasing one woman after another.

John Denton resided in San Francisco. [I left my heart…, in San Fran…cis…co…. Ha, ha ha! I must have gotten carried away. That song made me want to show off my heavenly choir voice. A harp would be great in the background, don't you think? I can hear it now. We angels love to sing some of your earthly songs, too!]

Oh well, enough sentimentality: let's get on with the story! Mr. Denton was an artist who painted and had many showings of his work in local art galleries. At night he went out to the bars and picked up many a woman as if there was going to be a shortage of them. In the end, however, he didn't want to get too tied down. For him, falling in love would have been too risky. I happened to pay a visit to him one cool rainy evening. He was in his studio working on one of his latest creations. I blew his window open and took him by surprise.

"What the hell was that? The winds are sure strong tonight. I'll just slam this shut. There, that should do it. Now I need to get back to my painting."

I flew nearer to him and hovered while he was working away. His thoughts were going a mile a minute. He sounded sort of lonely.

28

"It sure does get lonesome here. There's no lady to be with me. I guess I'm missing female companionship. They're fun in bed, but I thought that I'd never want one permanently." *He sighed.* "Oh well, I'd better get on with this painting. I'm having a show this weekend." *John continued working on his canvas and tried to shake off thoughts of falling in love.*

The following evening, there was a reception for his paintings. It was a fairly good crowd. Most people came by, grabbed some small glasses of wine and munched on crackers along with slices of gourmet cheese. It was then that events were about to change for Mr. Denton. In walked a lovely lady. She immediately drew his attention. She had long blond hair, a slim body and a pretty figure. Well, it looked like John's male hormones were working overtime.

"Wow! What a chick! I'd love to get her in bed." *These male humans are all alike. And he was going to get his wish, for the lady came up to him.*

"Hi! I Just love your paintings. You're rather talented. The colors you chose are really bright with a brilliant shine to them."

He felt very complimented. "Thank you. I have worked very hard at it, Miss...?"

"Baker..., I'm Janet Baker." *He grew more interested in her.*

"What brings you here to my modest little showing?"

"It so happens I'm doing a fashion show. I'm a

model for a prominent agency which brought me here to San Francisco."

"How long will you be in town?"

"Just for two weeks." *Her smile captivated him.*

"Have you ever had a portrait of yourself painted before?" '

"Why no, I never have. Why do you ask?"

"You would look very lovely on canvas. You being a model is an asset, along with your beauty."

"Well, since you mentioned it, I did have a secret wish to have my portrait painted someday."

"Great, how would you like me to paint you?"

"Really? I'd love you to."

"When would you like to start?" *I could see he was getting more anxious.*

"Tomorrow night would be fine, if that's OK."

"Great! Here is my card with my address. I'll see you then."

John was overjoyed with the prospect of having this wonderful, attractive model alone to himself. He thought about nothing else all next day. That evening she arrived at promptly at six and knocked. When he opened the door, he beheld her as she stood there.

"You look rather stunning tonight."

"Why, thank you!" *She blushed slightly at his kind words.*

"Here is my hot seat, you might say. I'll take your jacket for you." *She walked over the chair, sat down and posed for his painting. He could not keep his eyes off her, nor she likewise to him.*

30

An hour had elapsed and he suggested they take a break. She agreed. She looked at his work so far and she loved it. "My! This painting of me is coming along fine for such a short period of time."

"Oh, it's nothing," he said, displaying a bit of arrogance mixed with the expected modesty. "It just takes talent and the touch of the brush in the hand of an expert like me. Before you know it, voilà! --- my painting of you! By the way, would you like a glass of wine, my dear? You know, to loosen up a bit?"

"Yes, please. I just love wine."

"I have some white wine. Would that be OK with you?"

"I'd love it!" They both took a few sips and began kissing over and over. Bob asked if she would like to remove her dress and maybe pose in the nude for rest of the sitting. Being so relaxed from the wine she agreed and before you know it, he took his clothes off, too.

Janet grinned slyly. "I have a kinky idea. How about if I paint that hard cock of yours?"

A look of fear gripped John's face. "Not with this oil paint, you don't! I do happen to have some specially formulated body paint for that purpose. I'll get it for us right away."

When he had laid out the assorted colors of body paint, she took a little of the red and ever so gently brushed the tip of his dick. Giggling, she delved into the pink, yellow, green and orange, painting a series *of stripes up and down his shaft.*

After getting a few good laughs from this unusual activity, he begged her to wash it off so that they could go into his bedroom and get down to some serious screwing.

After that first night Bob saw more of Janet as the two weeks went by. Her days were full, and they could only get together in the evening. In no time at all their final night together arrived.

"My modeling gig here is coming to an end." *She held him tightly, and John felt so sad and disappointed. Then she sat on his lap and took off her bra, smiling at him all the while.*

"Why do you look so happy? I'm torn up inside at the thought of you going away."

"The thought of leaving tore me apart, too, so I requested to work for one of the agency's local offices here. I'm not going anywhere. That means I'm all yours, so come and get me."

Well, Bob could hardly believe what she had just told him. He had finally let the love bug bite and he no longer cruised the bars nor lived the life of a playboy. Love had once again triumphed.

By the way, I just love San Francisco. And that reminds of another song: hit it, Maestro!

> If you're going to San Francisco,
> There's gonna be some loving there!
> [*Hee hee hee!*]

SIX

You know, there is an attribute that we angels love to put into practice: it's that of a positive aura which we have. We always think positive; after all, we do reside up in the heavenly realm where our Creator lives. This brings to memory a past case I'd like to share with you.

In the suburbs of Cleveland, Ohio, there lived a woman named Betty Abrams. She was in her mid-sixties. She was a very negative person, always complaining. Everything was nothing but doom and gloom to her. People did not like to be around her because she always spoke very pessimistically about people and her life. Even flowers and plants died when they were around her! It was from the negative vibes she was giving out.

One sunny day Betty was out tending to her vegetable garden. She noticed that things were not growing, but actually dying.

"Oh, damn! They're all dying. It figures. I probably got bad seeds. I'll go over to that store and give them a piece of my mind!"

When she went to water some of her flowers, they too began to droop. "Shit! Not these! Christ, everything happens to me!"

While she was fuming, I sent a little birdie her way. It landed on her shoulder. At first she wanted to shoo it away or take a swat at it. Next, I tried to get her attention on a positive note. With the rub of my wing and hand, the birdie began to sing. Betty was astonished.

"Oh, my God! I've never heard a bird sing like that before." *She noticed that it was singing an actual song. It sounded like "When the Red Robin Comes Bobbin' Along." She was mesmerized and even sang along with the birdie. [By the way, it actually was a red robin. Sort of cute, huh?!]*

After this, I performed some visual effects of nature and directed them her way. Some butterflies flew all around her and a couple landed on her left shoulder.

"Wow amazing! I never had them land on me like this before." *She wanted to shoo them away, but Betty took in all of their beauty. To continue my magical performance, I simply touched her plants and flowers and they came alive. She stood there totally amazed and tried to shake herself awake, for she felt maybe she was daydreaming.*

For my next feat, I pointed her towards clouds forming in the sky. They looked like a smiley face looking down at her. And for my grand finale, I waved towards the sky and a bright sun appeared. The entire area where she stood was warm and it had the aura of calm, blissful joy.

Betty was enthralled by the atmosphere around her. It was so overwhelming that she sat down on the grass, taking everything in. But this was not all that had taken place. While she was sitting on the grass a man came walking by her. He was tall and thin with short red hair and the biggest smile you ever saw. He greeted her warmly.

"Hi there, how are you today?" *Betty glanced over and immediately took a liking to him.*

"I'm doing fine."

Betty raised herself up from the ground and walked over to the gentleman.

"I was just walking by and you caught my eye. You're such a lovely looking lady, so I'd thought I would say 'hi!' By the way, my name is Jack Benson, and yours?"

"I am Miss Betty Abrams. Thank you for stopping by, and for your lovely comments. I really don't get many visitors. It seems that no one ever comes around to see me."

"Really? Why is that?"

Betty began falling back into her usual negative routine about life and herself. This did not stop Jack from talking about positive things in life. She complimented him on how slim and nicely built he was. "Well, thank you. I take my daily strolls every day to keep fit, you know."

"You look like you can put some more meat there on those bones."

"I don't cook much. I make a mess of things in the kitchen."

Then I whispered an idea into Betty's ear. "How would you like come over to my place sometime? I'll make you a good home cooked meal. It looks like you could use one."

35

"Well! That would be wonderful. I can sure use a lady's touch in my life."

"How about tomorrow afternoon around 4:30?"

"Love to. See you then!"

Well! It looked as if Betty's tune had changed. She had learned that it's better to be positive in life and not a naysayer. The following afternoon Jack came over and Betty prepared a nice meal for him: a scrumptious pork roast with apple stuffing and all the trimmings: garlic mashed potatoes, honey-glazed carrots and a Caesar salad, topped off with cherry cobbler for dessert.

"Boy! I haven't eaten like this in a long time. It's fit for a king!"

After dinner they went into her living room and talked some more. Betty asked what he did for a living.

"I'm retired. I used to work for a law firm and had a partner. We were Benson and Dobbs."

She kept looking over at him and soon invited him to sit next to her. They held each other's hand and began kissing. Soon the sun was going down. They walked out onto her patio to watch the sunset. As they went back into her house they held each other. Betty felt love and warm tenderness as she had never felt before.

Well, you can guess for yourself what happened next. I'll just close her bedroom door. [My, but they're sure going at it, aren't they?] A full moon rose in the sky and one could hear the hoot of an owl. It was a night of all positive vibes: something all you humans need. Oh, and we angels, too!

SEVEN

I find it very interesting how you humans grow and raise your families. Each family and siblings are raised differently due to your location or your culture. It's quite unique. There was a case which comes to my mind. Take, for instance, Caroline.

She was twenty-one and had been living for quite a long time at home. Her parents had encouraged her to go out and experience the world for herself. The only drawback was that she was sheltered. All of her decisions were made for her.

She was very pretty with long dishwater blond hair. Caroline had really big blue eyes. Some nicknamed her "Bright Eyes." She lived with Edward and Judith Randolph in a cottage in Plainsville, Ohio.

She did have one attribute which benefited her. She was very honest and could not ever tell a lie. There were other things, however, which worked against her; she was gullible, naïve, too innocent, about life. Caroline was sweet and amiable, but she had a lot to learn about the world, especially concerning men. There were a lot of men out there ready to take advantage of such a lovely girl. They were like wolves intent on devouring her.

That is where I came in. I guided her along, but at some point she had to learn to be on her own and trust her own wisdom and intuition.

Let's take a peek now, and see what happened on her first day out on her own. At first she was nervous, unsure of herself. This was quite normal for a single young lady out in the world. She decided to look for a place to rent and found one. It was located in town, a house with room and board, "The Scenic Hideaway." Caroline paid in advance for everything and left her belongings in her room while she went out for a walk around town to see the sights.

She fell in love with the corner café and especially the women's clothing store, "Mary's Elegant Lady." She peeked through their window and something grabbed her eye immediately. She had been in the market for a new outfit, and this store would fit her needs perfectly. She walked into the shop and there she saw a woman who was busy stocking the shelves.

"Hello, my name is Mandy, how may I help you?"

"I would love to try on the nice outfit I saw in your shop window: the blue skirt with the white and yellow flowered blouse."

"Oh yes! They're both on sale. I'm sure you will love them and they should fit you perfectly."

"Do you have a dressing room?"

"Yes, it's over there in the corner. I'll help you try everything on."

She came out wearing her new outfit and looked herself over in the mirror. She was very pleased with what she saw.

"Why, this looks so lovely."

"Yes, you look simply stunning in it."

"I'll take it."

"Would you like me to wrap it up for you?"

"No, I'll just keep it on, it's so wonderful."

"The boys in town will just go crazy when they see you in that. Hahaha!"

Caroline was all excited about wearing her new dress. "What a nice way to start the first day on my own." *She decided to continue her little stroll around the town to get her bearings. At one point in her walk she decided to take a break, sitting down on a nice little white bench. Next to it was an old-fashioned street lamp. After a short while a handsome looking man in his early twenties sat down next to her. He had black wavy hair. He looked over at her, gave her a little flirty smile and winked at her. She looked back with her big bright eyes and smiled.*

"Hello, how are you?"

"I'm fine. Just sitting here taking a break."

"You're looking very pretty today."

She blushed. "Why thank you. How wonderful of you to say that."

"Oh, by the way, my name is John. Most people call me John-John. What's yours?"

"It's Caroline."

"That's such a wonderful name. What are you up to today?"

"I just moved out on my own and am living by myself."

"Really? How would like me to show your around the town?"

"That would be just wonderful."

"I know a nice place. Do you like ice cream? We

can head over to 'The Frosty Bear.'" *They walked a few blocks, chatting all the way and reaching the place in no time. They sat down and a waitress with JILL on her name tag came to their table.*

"What would you two like to order?"

"I'll have a hot fudge sundae."

"I'll have the same, please. Nice place isn't it? The ice cream is out sight." *Jill the waitress soon came back with their sundaes. They both dug in and enjoyed each other's company. John paid the bill when they were done. He suggested that they take a little walk in the park.*

"What are you doing this evening, Caroline?

"I have no plans at the moment."

"How would you like to go out to dinner with me?"

Her face lit up with joy. "I'd love to!"

"Great. How about around six? I'll come by and pick you up. Where do you live?"

"I'm staying over at a room and board called 'The Scenic Hideaway.'"

"Oh! I know the place." *He gave her a peck on the cheek, and she turned and kissed him back.* "I have to go now, see you later tonight." *They kissed again. Caroline was all excited: her first day on her own, and already she was asked out by a nice looking man.*

That evening, she decided to wait outside a few minutes earlier than six o'clock. Six rolled around, but there was no John. The clock began to tick away and ten to fifteen minutes had passed with still no John.

She was getting worried, not knowing why he did not come to get her. She decided to go over to the ice cream parlor to see if he might be there. She arrived and peeked into the window. Sure enough, he was with another woman. They were holding hands, and soon had their arms around each other. Caroline was heartbroken and felt very sad.

She walked back to the boarding house, went to her room and flopped on her bed. She cried and felt very lonely. I arrived in the room, blew a gentle breeze in her face and spoke to her mind:

Don't worry! There are men who are playboys,
   just going from one woman to another.

"It's a good thing that I found this out now," *she thought to herself*. "Imagine what would have happened if I had fallen in love with him. I'll be careful next time and wait for Mr. Right to come along."

I spoke to her mind again:

You've got it!
Good for you.

Caroline dated several men and learned by hit-and-miss until she finally found the right man. I knew she could do it on her own. It's better when you humans learn to trust yourselves and rely on your instinct.

42

EIGHT

Oh, excuse me! I must have been daydreaming. I was just sitting on top of a cloud here, imagining myself as Queen of the Nile. It must have been fun to have those slaves around, serving one's every whim. But I have learned to be myself. I am, after all, in the afterlife --- which brings another case to mind.

There was a young teenage girl named Julie Rutherford. She lived in Santa Monica, California, and attended Santa Monica High School. Among the students they called it SaMoHi! She lived at home with her parents, Ted and Susan Rutherford.

Julie was rather lonely. She always admired other girls. They always got all the dates. Even in her classes she was the last to be called. She thought everyone was better than her. Most of her classmates had a talent they excelled in, but she didn't. She felt that when it came to talents, they had passed her by.

When she was in class Julie would always daydream. This helped her escape reality and she did not have to face herself. There were idols in her life and when she met a movie star or celebrity she would get all excited. She was a carbon copy of Ethel Mertz from "I Love Lucy." [That's one of my favorite shows!]

She had a hero which was Marilyn Monroe. One day she came to school wearing a blond wig, dressed provocatively and speaking exactly like her idol. That day she sat in class and she talked in a Marilyn Monroe voice.

"Hello darling! Did you see me in my latest movie, 'The Seven Year Itch?' I had the grandest of times --- simply marvelous, my dear!"

Some of the guys whispered to each other, "Hey, will ya get a load of her! Who does she think she is, Marilyn Monroe?" Bill Bates, the history teacher came in and started the class.

"Good morning, everyone. Has everyone read chapter twelve, 'The Civil War'?" He looked over at Julie and asked her individually if she had read the chapter. She answered in her Marilyn Monroe voice," Why yes, my darling. I found it to be simply wonderful. By the way, how did you like me in the movie, 'Gentlemen Prefer Blondes'?"

The whole class including the teacher tried to keep from laughing. He didn't have the nerve to tell her that she was making a spectacle of herself. Poor girl, she was trying so hard to be like someone else. When will she ever learn to be herself? She was fifteen, and it was about time she did. I decided to pay her a visit later that day after dinner.

That entire day in school she spent acting just like her hero. When she was in the cafeteria, Julie ordered her lunch as Marilyn. The people who worked behind the counter and those in line snickered; they were not laughing with her, but at her. She thought she was being entertaining, but they didn't want to hurt her feelings. A girl standing next *to her in line almost dropped her tray full of food, she was trying to keep from laughing.*

When she got home, she was still dressed like her hero. Her mother greeted her as she came through the door.

"Hi, Julie!"

Her daughter blinked seductively and greeted her in her Marilyn Monroe voice. "Hello there, Mother dear. It's so nice to see you."

The mother looked at her rather oddly. "Why are wearing that wig along with that lipstick? And why, for Heaven's sake, are you talking like that?"

"Oh, I just adore Marilyn Monroe. I rented some her movies. I'm going to watch her in 'Some Like It Hot.' Call me when dinner's ready. *She breezed up the stairs, singing like Marilyn Monroe*:

"Happy birthday to you…
Happy birthday to you…
Happy birthday, Mister President,
Happy birthday to you!"

Her mother was quite concerned about her daughter. The father came home and his wife told him all about Julie. He merely laughed. "That's just a phase she's going through. We all had our heroes and heroines when we were growing up. I liked Jimmy Cagney and Humphrey Bogart. 'Play it again, Sam!' Ha ha!!"

"You may be right, dear. I loved Rock Hudson. He

was such a hot looking man!"

"Hey! What about me?! I've been told I have that Hudson profile!" *They both laughed.* "It looks like we're both over the hill."

"You can say that again!"

That evening Julie came down for dinner. This time she was all made up and did her usual Monroe shtick. "Thank you, Mr. President, for inviting me to dinner here at the White House. *She blew a kiss towards her father and shook hands and addressed her mom.* "It's so nice to meet you too, Mrs. Kennedy, you do have such elegant taste in decor."

Mrs. Rutherford stirred. "Okay, Julie, you can come back down to earth."

Mr. Rutherford frowned. "And I am not President Kennedy either. I am your father."

She held off with the voice and replied normally, "Okay, Daddy!" *They both told her she was overdoing it and suggested she find a different hobby or something else with which to occupy her mind. They began eating their meal: Porterhouse steaks, homemade fries and a Caesar Salad. For dessert there was pineapple upside down cake. When they finished their meal, Julie ran upstairs to her room. She closed the door and watched a movie with Marilyn Monroe. She began repeating her words from the movie and trying to emulate her.*

I believed it was high time for me to pay her a visit. She needed my help desperately before she'd go too far off the deep end. I had to figure out what would be a good entrance. Ah-ha! I got it! I saw that she had her bedroom window open. I just flew right in! Next, I made the whole area a little warmer, especially right where she was standing. I whooshed by so quickly that one of my feathers floated her way. She was astonished. "Wow! A large white feather! I wonder where it came from?" *I allowed her to feel my presence --- just a bit, not too much. I didn't want to scare her. She looked around and called out.* "Who's there? Funny, I thought there was someone standing next to me."

I flew on over to her computer and turned it on. It took her by surprise. "What's going on here? I've never had my computer start all by itself before!" *Scratching her head, she walked over to her desk, trying to figure it all out. Then I directed her internet to turn on to Youtube. Being ever so careful I whispered into her ear*:

Look up Marilyn Monroe
and her last days.

She did just as I had instructed: she sat quietly and watched a biography of Marilyn Monroe. Next, she saw below in the lineup a TV movie about her idol and clicked on it: "Marilyn Monroe: The Untold Story." Julie sat still and was glued to her computer. After watching the entire presentation she sat dumbfounded.

"Oh, my goodness! I never knew she had all those

problems. It seems like she didn't have a happy life: the loss of her mother, mental problems, several marriages, and on top of all that she was found dead from an overdose of sleeping pills."

Julie was stunned and didn't know how to take it all in. Very gently I spoke to her mind and it all began making sense to her.

"I understand now. She was human, just like me. She had all those problems, too." *Then I spoke again and it became even clearer and made her think.* "Would I like to be like her? I don't think so. I'd better just be me, and be thankful for who I am."

I blew another feather her way. A burst of cool air came through the window and a little birdie jumped on her window sill. It then jumped on her shoulder. "Wow! How fantastic can this be?" *She smiled.*

The next morning Julie came down to breakfast before she went off to school. This time she appeared as herself, not even speaking in a Marilyn Monroe voice. Her mother was surprised.

"What happened to Marilyn?"

"Oh, her? I decided that it's better to be myself. I found out that she was just human after all. Besides, she didn't have a very happy life, went through several men and had a tragic ending. They found her dead from an overdose of sleeping pills. I don't want that to ever happen to me."

Her mother was elated. "It's better for me to be myself, Mom, and no one else." *After breakfast, she saw her daughter off to school. She attended school that day as herself. In her creative writing class she and her fellow students were told to write any type of story, but to include something personal about themselves. She wrote her story and her teacher decided that it was so good that he had it published in the next edition of the school newspaper. It was entitled "Marilyn and Me."*

Julie finally discovered her gift was writing. She was being herself and not portraying someone else in order to be happy. She decided to major in English, continued writing and went on to become a famous novelist. She even made it on the bestseller list.

What's that? I hear a song coming from down there. It's from a large stadium and man is playing his piano: "A Candle in the Wind, Good Bye, Norma Jean." How apropos, don't you agree?

EPILOGUE

Well, it looks like my time is just about up. I need to attend to other humans down there. I hope that after reading all of my stories you took something of significance with you. Now you know how some of us angels work and intervene in the human experience. All of you have your own guardian angel. Some of us protect, advise and operate with many functions.

Remember, the next time you see a white feather, some unusual phenomenon occur right next to you or sometimes a soft voice speak to your conscience --- it's one of us!

I have been really blessed to have spent this time with you. Till we meet again, either there on earth or somewhere in the afterlife --- ta-ta!

Made in the USA
Columbia, SC
13 February 2024

31350292R00030